To Chaucer, the greatest nibbler of all —B. F.

For my dear friend Patty —A. N. K.

Published by Roaring Brook Press
Roaring Brook Press is a division of Holtzbrinck Publishing Holdings Limited Partnership
120 Broadway, New York, NY 10271 · mackids.com

Text copyright © 2022 by Beth Ferry
Illustrations copyright © 2022 by A. N. Kang

Library of Congress Control Number: 2021026410
ISBN 978-1-250-76241-2

Our books may be purchased in bulk for promotional, educational, or business use.
Please contact your local bookseller or the Macmillan Corporate and Premium Sales Department
at (800) 221-7945 ext. 5442 or by email at MacmillanSpecialMarkets@macmillan.com.

First edition, 2022 · Book design by Aram Kim and Melisa Vuong
The illustrations for this book were created digitally.
Printed in China by Hung Hing Off-set Printing Co. Ltd., Heshan City, Guangdong Province

1 3 5 7 9 10 8 6 4 2

NO NIBBLING!

GARDENERS KNOW
ALL THE DIRT!

Words by Beth Ferry   Art by A. N. Kang

Roaring Brook Press
New York

One warm spring day, Derwood planted a garden.

Dig.

Hoe.

Seed.

Sow.

Water.

Wait.

Grow, grow.

On that very same day, he noticed a dandelion puff.

It was early in the season for dandelions, but Derwood was taking no chances.

Growing a garden was risky business.

There was chickweed and pigweed and crabgrass.

There were leaf chewers

     and sapsuckers

          and root feeders.

There were woodchucks and chipmunks and skunks.

Pickers and pluckers and nibblers.

It was unbearable!

(Although, when he thought about it, bears had never

really given him a problem.)

As Derwood inspected the dandelion puff, he realized it wasn't a weed.

It was a tiny bunny.

"You're not a dandelion," Derwood said.

"Oh, no," squeaked the bunny. "I'm Tabitha. Are you growing vegetables?"

"Vegetables?" Derwood repeated. "Nonsense. I am conducting a very scientific dirt experiment. Very brown. Very boring. No vegetables growing here. Not one."

"Aw shucks," said the bunny.

Derwood firmly shut the garden gate.

Then he hurried home to sort his pest-control books by color.

A few weeks later, as the peas were climbing their posts . . .

"Hello, Mister Derwood," Tabitha said. "Mama sent me out for a morning **stalk**."

Derwood quickly inspected his cornstalks.

He scrutinized his celery stalks.

He examined his beanstalks.

Then he studied Tabitha.

"Why would I munch on . . . I mean, mention a **stalk**? I just walked over to see—"

"Nothing! Nothing to see here. If you'd like to see something, I suggest you head on over to the Very Far Away Berry Patch. They'll have something to see."

"I'd **butternut**, Mister Derwood. Mama said I'd **butter bean** home soon."

As Tabitha bounded away, Derwood counted every last bean.

He wasn't taking any chances.

Plus, counting beans was one of his favorite things to do.

Derwood forgot about the bunny in the busy summer days of weeding and staking and pruning.

As his tomatoes ripened, a rabbit hopped by.

"Hello, Mister Derwood," the rabbit said.

"Tabitha? Is that you? You're all grown up."

"I **yam**," said Tabitha. "And so is your magnificent garden."

"I know! Isn't it wonderf— Wait one minute.

Did you just say **yam**?"

"Um...no?"

"I may have misunderstood, but please understand, there can be no nibbling."

"Okey dokey," said Tabitha. "**Lettuce** talk about something else."

"Did you just say **lettuce**?"

"Of course not. I said, let us talk about the weather."

Derwood *loved* talking about the weather.

He was an expert on clouds and hadn't had a satisfying conversation about precipitation in a very long time.

Guarding a garden was lonely work, and despite that twitching nose, Tabitha seemed like a good listener. Her ears were big enough.

Plus, she seemed to know a lot about vegetables.

"I do think it's going to rain tomorrow," Derwood said. "Those nimbus clouds look promising."

"Ooh," said Tabitha, "I love a good **squash** in the rain."

"Did you just say **squash**?"

"Heavens, no. I said I love to wash in the rain. Don't you?"

"Goats don't really enjoy the rain," Derwood admitted. "But it is good for the garden."

"Rabbits don't really **carrot** one way or another."

"Excuse me? Did you just say **carrot**?"

"Oh, Mister Derwood, why would I say crunchy, delicious **carrot**?"

"Hmm," said Derwood. "Isn't it time for you to be getting home? I have a few things to do."

"I **beet** you do," said Tabitha.

"State your intentions, herbivore!"

"**Lima** nothing but a friendly rabbit hoping for some nice, refreshing . . . conversation.

You are **turnip**ing my words all around."

Derwood turned as red as his tomatoes, followed by an alarming shade of eggplant.

"**Romaine** calm, Mister Derwood. Please sit down and rest yourself."

"Rest myself? Derwoods don't rest. I must weed the rutabaga."

"You rest, Mister Derwood. I will weed the rutabaga."

Derwood could not believe his ears (which were not all that much smaller than Tabitha's).

"Did you just say you would weed?"

"Indeed!"

So Derwood rested,

relaxed,

reclined,

and secretly rejoiced as Tabitha
weeded his garden.

"Weeds are tricky!" Tabitha complained.

"Lots of things in a garden are tricky," Derwood agreed.

"Ooh, look at this one! I wish—"

"But my wish . . . ," Tabitha whispered.

"Weeds aren't wishes," Derwood scoffed. "Plus, *I* can make your wish come true."

"How?" asked Tabitha. "How could you know what my wish is?"

"Oh, Tabitha, I know. I've always known."

And then Derwood Goat, master gardener,

bean counter,

and cloud connoisseur,

granted Tabitha's wish.

"To nibble!" Derwood agreed.

Tabitha's nose twitched,

twitched,

double-twitched.

Then she sprouted a smile from ear to ear.

"Oh, thank you, Mister Derwood! Thank you very ..."

MUNCH!

CELERY

CABBAGE

PEAS

TOMATOES

CARROTS

CORN